The Weavers and the Elephant

HANSDA SOWVENDRA SHEKHAR is a writer and translator. He writes in English; and translates from Santali, Hindi and Bengali to English. He is the author of the novels, *The Mysterious Ailment of Rupi Baskey* and *My Father's Garden*; the collection of stories, *The Adivasi Will Not Dance*; and the books for children, *Jwala Kumar and the Gift of Fire*, *Who's There?* and *Sumi Budhi and Sugi*. He translated Manoj Rupda's Hindi novel, *Kaale Adhyaay*, into English as *I Named My Sister Silence*.

PROITI ROY is an illustrator for children's books. She studied fine arts in Viswa Bharati, Shantiniketan, West Bengal. She also taught children art and craft for 12 years. She had been a part of the advertising industry in Bangladesh and India before settling down with the idea of become an illustrator and graphic designer. Recipient of the Big Little Book Award in 2017, she has been working for publishers and NGOs who create books for children. She is also actively involved with animal welfare work in and around Shantiniketan, where she lives with her many rescued dogs.

Hansda Sowvendra Shekhar

The Weavers and the Elephant

Also featuring
Khikri Kata Bhoot &
Tina Quito and Tara Musca

RED PANDA

ILLUSTRATED BY PROITI ROY

Published by Red Panda, an imprint of Westland Books, a division of Nasadiya Technologies Private Limited, in 2025

No. 269/2B, First Floor, 'Irai Arul', Vimalraj Street, Nethaji Nagar, Alapakkam Main Road, Maduravoyal, Chennai 600095

Westland, the Westland logo, Red Panda and the Red Panda logo are the trademarks of Nasadiya Technologies Private Limited, or its affiliates.

ISBN: 9789371979405

10 9 8 7 6 5 4 3 2 1

Book design by Saurabh Garge

Printed at Parksons Graphics Pvt. Ltd

IN MEMORY OF MY CHILDHOOD

IN KISHORIPUR AND MOUBHANDAR

—SOWVENDRA

The Elephant from the Sky

Many, many years ago

By the river Sorna
There was a village
And it was the most beautiful village
One had ever seen.
There were trees
There were meadows and orchards
And all over grass green.

It was a village of weavers
Who lived in houses built along a dirt track.
Their houses were beautiful.

On their looms

the weavers created

cloth and fabrics

This cloth was later used by tailors in the town
to create dresses.

The weavers used yarns and threads of several colours
The yarns were rich and pretty,
As pretty as the village the weavers lived in.
The weavers went to the market in the town to sell their cloth and fabrics
The people at the market liked their fabrics and they paid a good price.

The weavers
were prosperous
except one weaver
in the village.

This weaver was perhaps
the poorest weaver
in the village

She lived in a small
cottage outside the village
With her old parents
and a very young sister.

She had been unable to find a partner for marriage
As she was considered ugly
And because she was not married,
She was teased by the other weavers of the village.
'She's a curse,' they said
'A grown-up woman still sitting
in her father's house.'
'She's a burden,' they said,
pretending to be concerned
'Wonder if
her unfortunate shadow
will ruin her
sister's
prospects too'.

But that was not the fact
The weaver was perhaps the most hardworking one
in the village
It was her hard work that ran the household,
For her parents were old, sick and unable to work.
And there were so many challenges to face.
While all the other weavers had good looms
to work on

The poor weaver had
one old,
rickety loom

Which she was
finding hard
to maintain.

It was difficult to run that loom,
To oil it
To make it work properly.
So, most of the poor weaver's resources
Were spent in maintaining her loom
And she never had enough money
To buy good yarn.
As a result,

The fabric the poor
weaver created
Was not as good as
the fabrics created
by the
rich weavers.

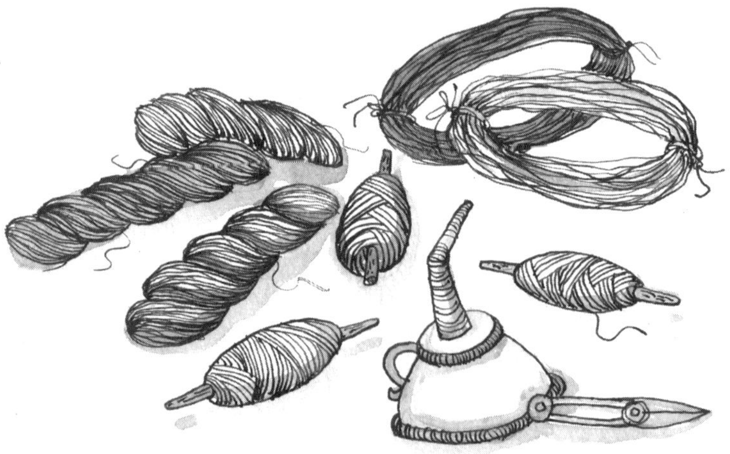

At the market in the town,
The rich weavers found wealthy customers
And they purchased the best, most
expensive yarns
To create fabrics.

The poor weaver could
sell her fabric
Only to customers who were
as poor as her.

And she barely earned
enough money
To buy both an ordinary yarn and provisions
for her family.
Yet, that poor weaver lived a happy and satisfied life
With whatever she earned
And she sought
nothing more.

She had once tried asking help from the rich weavers
But they did not help her.
Instead, they laughed at her and barred her from entering their street: 'Do not bring your unlucky self near our homes anymore.'
Since that day
the poor weaver asked
no one for help
And made do with whatever she earned.

She lived happily in her small cottage outside
the village
Surrounded by greenery
And the sound of the flowing Sorna.
Though the weavers had been living in the village for
a long time
What they did not know was that
The beauty of their village
had long been attracting
a visitor from the Sky
It was the
Elephant from the Sky
The Elephant
from the Sky
had wings
like a butterfly's.

Sheer, but strong.
He came flying down from the Sky every night
Grazed in the meadows
Ate fruits from the trees
Splashed around
in the cool, clean water
of the Sorna.
And,
Just before
the night came
to an end,
Flew

Up

Up

Up

Up into the Sky

One night,
The poor weaver heard someone playing in the Sorna
And went out of her house to investigate.
What she saw took her breath away.

There was
an elephant
Whose skin was
bright blue
in colour
And who
had wings with
rainbow colours

Who had ever seen an elephant with wings?
But there it was,
right in front of the poor weaver's eyes—
an elephant with wings
playing in the river.
The weaver was scared
But she was also very curious
So, she went closer
to the elephant to enquire.

The elephant played all night long
The poor weaver saw the elephant play all night long
And, as the elephant was leaving just before daybreak,
The poor weaver caught his tail.

The Elephant

from the Sky

flew Up

Up

Up.

And along with him,
the weaver too went

Up

Up

Up.

Up
into
the Sky

Into a land of magic

Of strange
trees and landscapes
And a lot of yarns.

Yes, yarns.

The poor weaver could not believe her eyes.

There were yarns

in all colours, all textures,

So much that

it defied her imagination.

These were the kind of yarns that no one on earth had seen
Whether in their village or elsewhere
It was a treasure of yarns.
Though the weaver was a simple, honest woman
She could not help bundling a few balls of yarn in the end of her sari
Just to try them out on her loom.
At night, when

the Elephant from the Sky flew

Down

Down

Down

The poor weaver caught his tail
and flew back to her village.
To her home
To her loom
And she began
working eagerly.

'Where were you
the whole day?'
The poor weaver's sister
asked her
'I was so worried.
Baba and Ma were
sick again
What could I have done alone?
You know no one helps us'.
'We won't need
anyone's help anymore,'
The poor weaver
assured her sister
'The Sky has helped us'

And she told her sister
of her adventure.

The sister was certainly surprised
But she was more surprised when the weaver created
Magical fabrics from the yarns from the Sky.
On the next market day,
The poor weaver's fabrics became an instant hit

The rich customers
in the town
fought with one another
To buy the
poor weaver's fabrics.

Such popular
the poor
weaver's fabrics
had become.

The rich weavers were surprised to see the poor weaver's success.

But they were even more surprised when
they saw that
The poor weaver did not buy any new yarn
for herself.
Yet, on the next market day,
The poor weaver came to the market with even more
beautiful fabrics.
The rich customers flocked to her stall
And she was flooded with offers and deals.

Within a short time,
The poor weaver became the richest weaver
in the village

But she remained as simple as before.

All she did with the money was
Repair her rickety loom and
make it as good as new

And add two new rooms to
her cottage.
One, a better room
for her parents;
the other for her fabrics.

The rich weavers were

very jealous and very curious

About the richest weaver's achievements

'What does she have that we don't have?'

And so they started spying on her.

Of course, they found nothing

The richest weaver worked till evening
Then she had a meal with her family
And went off to sleep.
The spy of the rich weavers could not
Find anything amiss, as
he saw that the richest weaver was
merely following her routine.

So, once the richest weaver went to sleep,
He too went away without spying anymore.
Also, after having earned all that money,
the richest weaver had reduced
her visits to the Sky
So even if the spy spied on her
all day and all night,
There was nothing extraordinary
he could find out
As

the richest weaver
hardly needed
To come out
of her house
Unless
she needed to bring
more yarns from the Sky.

The richest weaver prospered,

and the rich weavers grew more envious

and more curious.

And they were totally disappointed in their spy

So they decided to spy on the richest weaver

themselves.

No matter how many hours or days it took them,

They were determined

to unearth her secret.

They spent nights

Outside the richest weaver's house

But nothing happened.
Then, one night,
When the richest weaver needed new yarns
She went to the riverbank.
The rich weavers followed her

And what they saw
made their jaws drop.

An elephant
Blue in colour
With butterfly wings
in rainbow colours
Frolicking in the Sorna.
And the richest weaver
flew to the Sky
Up
Up
Up.

'So this is what she is up to,'
The rich weavers said to one another
When they saw that the next night
The richest weaver came down to earth with armloads of yarns

The rich weavers told the secret to everyone
on their street
And it was decided that they would fly to the Sky
With the blue elephant that night.
Just after midnight,
all the rich weavers and their families
Gathered on the riverbank.

The Elephant
from the Sky
came down,
Roamed around
Frolicked.
And

Just as it began flying,
All the rich weavers and
their families
Held on to his tail
In this way.
First, the second-rich weaver,
who had started the mission
against the richest weaver,
Held on to
the Elephant's tail.
That weaver's wife
held on to him.
The third-rich
weaver held on
to the second-rich
weaver's wife.
And so they held on
Creating a long chain
Flying

Up

Up

Up

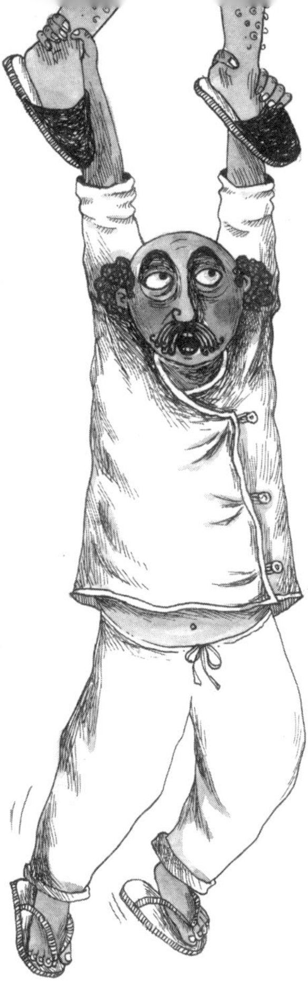

Holding on to the tail of the Elephant from the Sky.

All the weavers were very curious.

They just could not hold their excitement and curiosity.

One weaver, at the bottom end of the chain, asked the weaver holding the tail of the elephant 'Kette kette soota?

How much yarn did you say the richest weaver brought back?'

'Ette ette soota,
She brought back
this much yarn,'
The second-rich weaver
tried telling
the rich weaver
at the
bottom of the chain,
'How much yarn
did you say? I cannot
understand you,'
The curious weaver shouted back.
Irritated, the second-rich weaver
spread his arms to show
the armload of yarn
the richest weaver brought
'Ette ette soota!
This much yarn!'
And with that

The entire chain of rich weavers

Dropped the tail of the Elephant from the Sky

And fell down on earth.

Somewhere far, far from their village.

The rich weavers and their families did not return to their village anymore.

The richest weaver is now
the best weaver in the entire land.
She owns a clothing factory in the town and
several boutiques in several towns.
She makes expensive clothes for the royalty
and the rich and the famous.
And quality clothing at affordable prices
for those with just enough money.
And she donates clothes
to those who are unable to buy
In the memory of her parents
whom she lost not very long ago.
The business is managed by her
sister and they have several weavers
and tailors working for them
But
she prefers to live in
her small cottage
with two extra rooms
in her village.

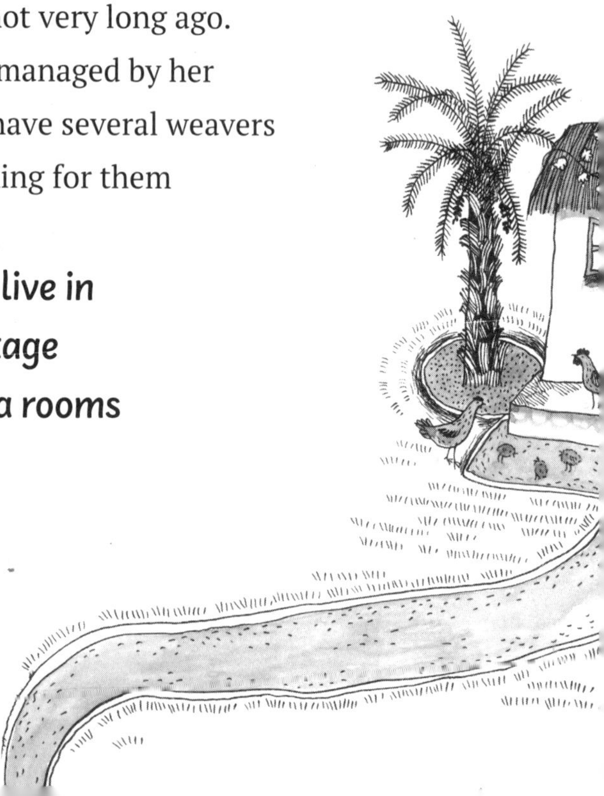

The insignia
of the business
of the richest weaver is

An Elephant with the
Wings of a Butterfly

Drawn in blue
and the colours
of the rainbow.

The Khikri-kata Bhoot

In another village by the river Sorna, very far from that village of weavers, there lived a wolf-legged ghost.

Those who had seen it claimed that it looked so terrible that they averted their gaze and instead looked at its legs—the legs of a wolf! And once they saw the ghost's wolf legs, they just ran away, fearing for their lives, for the ghost might just gobble them up or cause them some other harm, some other way.

In the language those villagers spoke, the word for wolf was khikri, the word for leg was kata, and the word for ghost was bhoot.

So, the **wolf-legged ghost** came to be known as **khikri-kata bhoot.**

No one knew where the khikri-kata bhoot lived. It just came out of thin air at dusk, when the sun had already set but it was not dark yet. It was the time when the villagers herded their children and their animals into their houses, for safety, because the khikri-kata bhoot had already stolen a number of goat kids, piglets, chicken, ducks, and at least one human baby, and apparently feasted on them.

Though no one knew where the khikri-kata bhoot lived, everyone believed that it lived on the top of a palm tree on the bank of the Sorna. At dusk, the khikri-kata bhoot stealthily climbed down the tree, made its way towards the village and pounced upon any prey it could find.

Then it dragged its prey to the top of the palm tree and feasted upon it there.

The villagers claimed that on several occasions they had seen bones of animals strewn beneath that particular palm tree on the bank of the Sorna. Those bones had made them believe that the khikri-kata bhoot lived on the palm tree. Such was their fear that people avoided going anywhere near that tree at all times of the day, and near the Sorna after sunset.

In that village lived a poor widow. She earned her living making earthen pots that she sold at the market in a town quite far away. The widow had a child, a daughter who was now ten years old but mature beyond her years because of their life of hardship.

While the mother worked at her wheel and went to the market, the little girl went to study in the village school in the morning and kept the house in her mother's absence in the afternoon, after returning from school. Though her mother did not allow her to touch the chulha, the girl could keep the house and the surroundings clean.

The woman and her daughter lived in a small hut by the Sorna. They were aware of the khikri-kata bhoot, but they could not move away from their house because they had nowhere else to go. The hut was on the ancestral land owned by the woman's dead husband, a property she steadfastly held on to, as she and her daughter would be left with nothing if they left that land. So the woman lived on her land despite being warned by the villagers of the khikri-kata bhoot.

As long as the woman stayed in the village, working in the house or at her wheel, she did not worry about her daughter. But when she went to the market to sell her wares, she warned her daughter sternly about staying safe.

'Do not be late from school.'

'Do not go out after sunset.'

'Keep the door latched and do not open it for anyone, even if you know them. Open the door only when I knock on it.'

To make sure that her daughter opened the door only for her, the woman had taught her a code.

'If you hear a knock on the door,' the woman instructed her daughter, 'ask: "What are you knocking for?" If it is me, I will answer: "Our wheel will catch a cold, so I want to put it inside the house." If you do not hear this answer, do not open the door, whatever happens.'

The daughter knew this lesson well. She did not need to be told again and again. And she also did not need to be told that the question and its answer was a secret between her mother and her—a secret never to be shared with anyone else.

Despite this, the woman was always afraid for her daughter. So, even if some of her wares were still to be sold at the market, she made sure to leave the town in the afternoon so that she could get back home before sunset.

But one evening, she could not reach home on time.

It had been raining heavily. The Sorna was flooded. The woman had set out for the market early in the morning, on a bullock cart. Its owner had agreed to carry her wares to the town, but she was not able to leave the market in the afternoon. It rained for a long time and quite heavily, so the woman had to shelter herself and her wares. And that delayed her.

When she finally got the opportunity to leave the market, it was still drizzling and she still had two unsold pots, which she tied together and lugged on her back.

But however fast she walked, she was still very far from her village when the sun set.

The woman looked dejectedly at the dark sky above her. A spray of raindrops hit her face and a little prayer escaped her lips:

'May my daughter be safe. That is all I ask for.'

At home, the little girl had shut all the doors and windows. She had returned home early from the school because of the rain. She lit a lamp and began practising the word problems they had been taught in the arithmetic class at the school that day. She was scared. Her mother had never been this late before, even during the rains. What was taking her so long? When would she come? When would she knock the door? The pitter-patter of the raindrops and the occasional thunder were making the girl even more nervous.

Then, suddenly ...

KNOCKKNOCKKNOCK!!!

The girl shivered and looked up from her notebook.

She listened closely.

Was it real? Was there really a knocking on their door?

KNOCKKNOCKKNOCK!

Yes, the knocking was real. The girl immediately ran to the sturdy wooden door and was just about to remove the heavy, horizontal beam of wood set against the door when her mother's lesson came back to her.

How stupid of me, the girl thought and immediately pulled her hands back. The wooden beam was ancient and very heavy and there was no way she would be able to put it back again quickly once she removed it from position. How would I save myself if it is the khikri-kata bhoot?

The girl stepped away from the door.

KNOCKKNOCKKNOCKKNOCKKNOCK!

The girl was drenched in sweat. She got a grip on herself and remembered her mother's lesson.

'What are you knocking for?' she asked hesitatingly, but loud enough for the one knocking on the door to hear.

There was no answer.

The girl crouched on the floor in terror.

There was silence all around. Even the pitter-patter of the raindrops seemed to have gone quiet.

Minutes passed. The girl kept staring at the door before her and waiting for the next knock.

Then, suddenly ...

KNOCK.

KNOCK.

KNOCK.

Three patient knocks. Not hurried knocks like before. Just three well thought out knocks.

Is that my mother? What if it is my mother?

No, something told the girl, this is not your mother. Your mother will answer your question.

But what if she is drenched and cold and just wants to enter the home soon?

No. Never. Your mother loves you. It is for a reason that your mother has devised the secret question. You would disobey your mother if you open the door for any stranger.

And so, the girl waited.

For another knock.

But there was silence.

And then, suddenly ...

KNOCKKNOCK KNOCKKNOC KKNOCK

KNOCK!

'What are you knocking for?'

The girl's voice this time was composed, confident and loud.

'I am your mother. Let me in. Such a terrible rain!'

The girl was alarmed.

The tone of the voice was annoyed, but the voice was her mother's.

Oh dear! My mother is getting drenched outside ...

The girl ran and placed both her hands on the horizontal wooden beam.

And then ...

WAIT WAIT WAIT ...

JUST WAIT! REMOVE YOUR HANDS FROM THE WOODEN BEAM.

The voice inside her head held the little girl back.

Ask that question once more. Just ask. You have not received the answer that you were expecting. So, ask. Ask. Don't hesitate. Your life depends on it. Ask.

And so, the girl asked again: 'What are you knocking for?'

This time, the voice from behind the door was kind: 'I am cold, my child. Open the door now.'

The voice was her mother's!

The girl asked herself, 'What do I do now? What if she really is my mother?'

Ask her another question, the voice inside her head told the girl. Your mother will only be happy to hear you asking so many questions for your own safety.

And so, the girl
thought of another question.

She asked: 'Mother, will you show me your feet? I want to see if the alta you applied in the morning is still there. If it has been washed off, I shall apply a fresh coat. I want you to enter the house only with feet painted with alta.'

The girl hit upon an idea. She would ask the one standing beyond the door to show their feet so she could see if they had the feet of a wolf. She knew her mother's feet well. Even if it were a human being knocking on the door, she could tell her mother's feet from any other person's. Also, the girl knew that her mother, being a widow, did not wear alta.

The girl watched in the dim light of the lamp ...

A human foot slid inside through the little gap beneath the door and the floor. The feet were slender and beautifully painted with alta.

The girl was convinced now that whoever was knocking on her door was certainly not her mother.

And then she looked closely.

The foot was human, but the talons were certainly not.

The foot had toes, but they did not have nails.

They had claws!

The girl now knew for sure that **the khikri-kata bhoot had changed its form to visit her.**

She shivered. In fright, in sorrow. She shivered. And then she got a grip on herself.

No, ***my mother has taught me to be brave and I will fight this ghost, the girl thought.***

She immediately thought of an idea. Even though she was not allowed to go near the chulha, she went to it and began blowing into it with a short iron pipe, just the way she had seen her mother do to light the embers.

In a few minutes, some of the embers started glowing. 'Open the door, child,' the khikri-kata bhoot called again in her mother's voice.

KNOCKKNOCKKNOCK!

'Just a moment,' the girl answered. 'I am looking for a stick to apply the alta on your foot. Just keep your foot there. Do not move it.'

The girl gathered some bright red, glowing embers in an aluminium ladle and ran and poured those embers on the khikri-kata bhoot's foot.

'AAWOOOOOOO ...'

A wolf's howl rose from beyond the door. It was so loud and frightful that the girl dropped the ladle and slumped to the ground, frozen with fear.

'WOOWOOWOO ...'

The khikri-kata bhoot could not immediately withdraw its foot. It howled again in agony, and the girl, saw something she would not forget very soon: the human foot turning into that of a wolf.

And the wolf foot dragged itself outside the door and the howls receded, far, far away.

For a long time, the girl sat frozen on the ground. And then, suddenly ...

KNOCKKNOCKKNOCK!

The girl was shaken out of her stupor.

But this time, she was alert and confident.

She asked loudly: 'What are you knocking for?'

And a voice, her mother's voice, answered patiently: 'Our wheel will catch a cold, so I want to put it inside the house.'

The girl was elated on hearing that answer. But she did not, like the last time, rush to open the door.

There were still some embers burning bright in the chulha. She carried some more in the ladle and placed those on the ground, near the door, from where she could pick those up easily. Only then did she begin removing the horizontal wooden beam. If it were anyone else and not her mother, they would have burning embers thrown on their face!

But no, it was indeed her mother. Both mother and daughter were so relieved to see each other that they began crying. The mother embraced her daughter tightly and the daughter would not let go of her mother.

And then the daughter told her mother all that had happened before she returned. And the mother was so happy and proud of her daughter that she hugged her again and they wept again.

After that day, somehow, no one in that village was ever attacked again by the khikri-kata bhoot.

The sunsets, the dusks, even the nights became peaceful and fear-free on that bank of the Sorna.

The khikri-kata bhoot seemed to have left the village. After some time, the palm tree on which it was said to live fell down on its own. The villagers were very happy. They too wept tears of joy and relief.

The mother–daughter perhaps knew why this had happened. But they kept it a secret, just like their secret question and its answer.

Tina Quito and Tara Musca

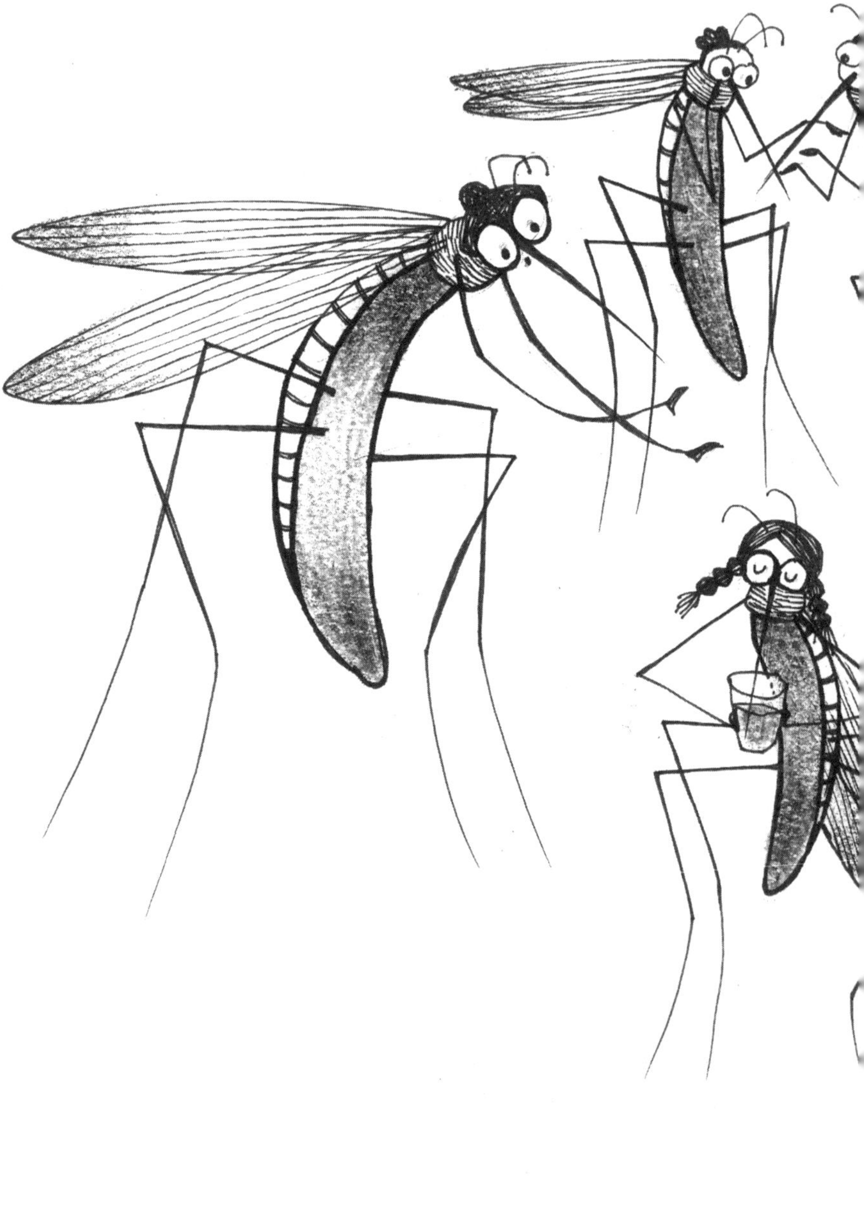

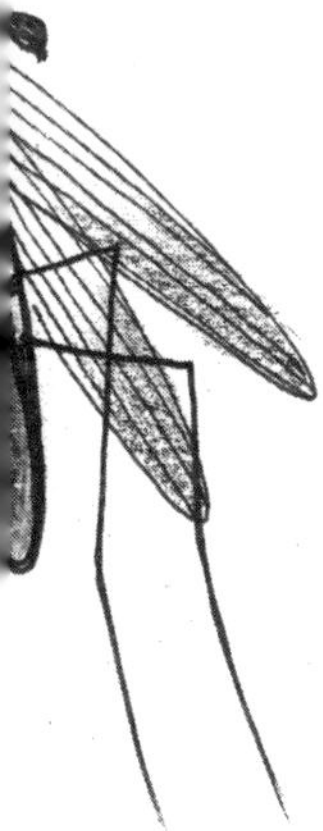

And at another place by the river Sorna, far away from the village of weavers and where no one had heard of the khikri-kata bhoot ...

The distraught Mrs. Nina Quito was shouting at her daughter, Tina.

'Oh! I am so sad! This girl will spoil everything and turn me into a laughing stock before everybody I know! Is this why I raised you and turned you into a big girl? So that you might feed yourself sugar syrup and not blood?'

Mrs. Nina Quito loved Tina, but all of Mrs. Nina Quito's friends were scandalised by Tina and that embarrassed Mrs. Nina Quito so much. All of Mrs. Nina Quito's friends called Tina "wayward", and that broke Mrs. Nina Quito's heart every time.

'Whoever has heard of a mosquito loving sugar syrup more than blood?' Mrs Mina Quito quipped.

'Something is wrong with their genes,' Mrs Rina Quito added. 'I always knew this family was odd.'

Hahahaha ... Mrs. Mina Quito and Mrs. Rina Quito laughed as they talked about Tina. And that plunged Mrs. Nina Quito into further gloom and embarrassment.

And that is why she screamed at Tina the moment she saw her perched on the edge of a plate on which sat two gulab jamuns, both covered with a generous serving of chashni or sugar syrup on which Ms Tina Quito had been feasting, yet unnoticed by the human for whom those gulab jamuns had been served.

'TINAAAA ... *are you listening to me?*'

Mrs Nina Quito shouted again, nearly tearing her microscopic throat out.

But would Ms Tina Quito listen to her mother?

Nope.

She just loved sugar syrup. It was for her the best liquid, the best food in the whole wide world, and she could spend her entire life just sucking on the sweet, thick syrup wherever she could find it. Mosquitoes were expected to feed on blood, but Ms Tina Quito would have none of it.

'No, no, no. Just no, no, no,' Ms Tina Quito had told her family and everyone who shamed her for not feeding on blood. 'I do not like blood. Do I need to write it down for you? I just do not like blood. It is not that I have any issue with our biting humans for blood and causing them pain or giving them diseases. I don't care about humans and their pain and I care nada about we mosquitoes having this image of disease-spreading parasites. I care only about myself, I like sugar syrup better and so I drink it whenever possible. If I don't find sugar syrup anywhere, I'll drink blood to stay alive. But if I find sugar syrup, I won't drink blood at all.'

'You are crazy!' Mrs Nina Quito said, even as her daughter flew away, her wings buzzing.

***

'This seems like a good spot to have sugar syrup.' Ms Tina Quito had spotted sugar syrup on a plate of lobongo lotika and immediately landed on the plate, in the middle of the sugar syrup.

There wasn't much syrup on the plate—it was lobongo lotika, after all, not gulab jamun or rasgulla—but it was thick enough.

Ms Tina Quito was sucking up the sugar syrup on the plate of lobongo lotika when she realised that she was unable to flap her wings anymore.

'Oh no! What have I got myself into? Who will help me out now?'

Ms. Tina Quito thought as the sugar syrup she had landed on started to cover her and pull her in. Whole.

She had been so busy filling herself with the delicious and satiating sugar syrup that she had completely forgotten about its texture. She realised that it wasn't thick enough to keep her afloat. She had started sinking. Her proboscis was buried deep in the syrup, her legs were stuck, her wings too had sunk, and the syrup—though not thick—was so sticky that she just could not move. Now there was only the sweetness of the sugar syrup in her mouth, a dazed feeling of probably not being alive anymore, and just one thought in her head: **'I am so lucky I got to taste such wonderful sugar syrup just before my death.'**

Ms Tina Quito closed her eyes and sucked in some more sugar syrup and waited for it to dissolve inside her mouth or for the sugar syrup to suck her in completely—whichever came first...

***

In a blink,

Ms Tina Quito

was up in the air!

The strong tug she felt in her thorax as something powerful lifted her up in the air made Ms Tina Quito open her eyes.

There was the world beneath her. The plate of lobongo lotika she had been sinking into just a few moments ago. The bald crown of the middle-aged man who was feasting on that lobongo lotika. The crowded restaurant, the familiar faces and utensils and counters and shelves, the place she frequented in search of sugar syrup. The place where she had thought she would die, but she hadn't. She was alive, still alive.

I'm alive?

I'm out of that sugar syrup bog?

But—but how?

She felt the grip on her thorax loosening and her body being lowered. She landed on the floor in a quiet corner of the restaurant. Whoever had carried her out of that sugar syrup bog, let go of her syrup-stained body.

Ms Tina Quito, more curious about who had rescued her than thankful for the fact that she had been rescued, immediately turned around to look at her benefactor. All she could see through her surprised, almost syrup-covered eyes were a blob far bigger than her; a grin that was so real and disarming; a pair of beautiful gossamer wings, prettier than her own; and—is it real? Am I seeing alright? She thought—something that looked like a coat-button daisy on top of that blob.

'Hi,' the blob smiled. 'I'm Tara. Tara Musca. You okay? Do you want to clean up? You mind if I lick that syrup off your body? You see, I love sugar syrup as much as you do.'

Ms Tara Musca had almost the same story to tell as Ms Tina Quito did. She too was criticised and judged and talked about day in and day out. Not for her diet, of course—houseflies are known for eating, and Ms Tara Musca was no different—but she was judged for her body. With her nearly roundish, blob-like look, Ms Tara Musca defied the chief beauty and body standard laid down in the canon of houseflies. She was stout, not slender.

'How does she even fly with that body?' Mr Rocky Musca, next-door neighbour and a most irritating vermin, commented every time he passed by Ms Tara Musca.

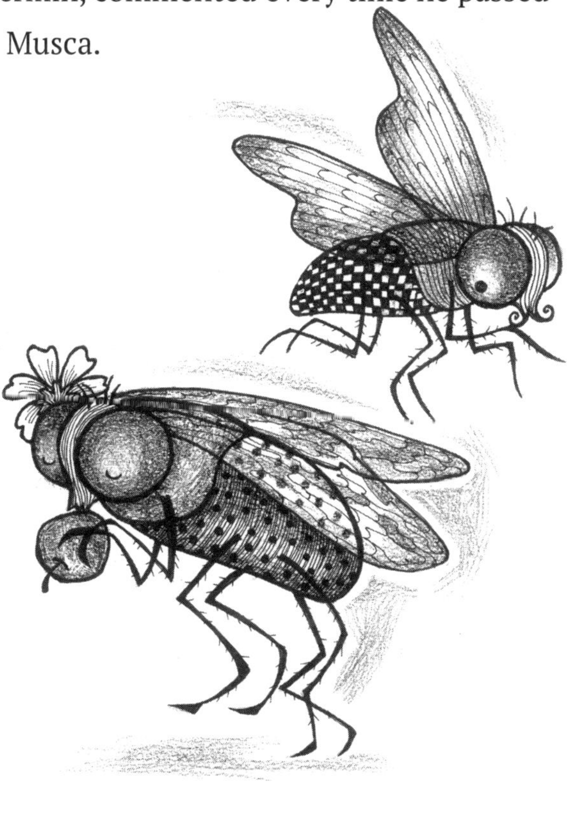

'Yo, brother,' seconded Mr Tocky Musca, another very irritating vermin. 'She could just drop somewhere and die. She could be crushed by that stupid flower she has on her head.'

Kick. Kickkickkickkick.

'Owww ...' Mr Tocky Musca groaned, having received a series of flying kicks from Ms Tara Musca. Ms Tara Musca had put all her weight behind those kicks, so they were nearly as heavy and strong as she was.

'What was that for?' Mr Tocky Musca asked, rubbing his head where Ms Tara Musca's flying kicks had fallen.

'For thinking that I would die that easily,' Ms Tara Musca said. 'Next time, show me some respect. Or else the kicks will be stronger. And that is not some stupid flower on my head. It's called a coat-button daisy. Remember the name.'

Mr Tocky Musca could not move for a few seconds. Those kicks had hurt quite hard. Mr. Rocky Musca flew away the moment he saw Mr. Tocky Musca falling down.

***

'I used to think I was the only one so crazy for sugar syrup,' Ms Tara Musca said to Ms Tina Quito, who was still surprised at having been rescued.

'Hello!' Ms Tara Musca waved a leg before Ms Tina Quito's eyes. 'But just look at you! You nearly gave up your life to drink sugar syrup! And you are—you are—a mosquito! Who has ever heard of a mosquito so crazy about drinking sugar syrup?'

'And who has ever heard of a housefly wearing a flower on her head?' Ms Tina Quito retorted.

'Oh! This?' Ms Tara Musca smiled her charming smile. 'I love flowers, actually. And this coat-button daisy is my absolute favourite. So, I wear it on my head.'

Ms Tina Quito smiled at Ms Tara Musca.

Ms Tara Musca smiled back at Ms Tina Quito. They could feel the warmth growing between them.

'I don't know how to put it,' Ms Tara Musca said, 'but I'm seen as quite an oddball by my community because my body is heavy and I wear a flower on my head. I mean, how do I change my body? What stupid exercises should I do and what stupid foods should I stop eating? And I love flowers. How is it wrong to love flowers?'

'That's okay,' Ms Tina Quito said. 'You're only an oddball. I'm seen as someone utterly wayward by my community because I love drinking sugar syrup and prefer it over drinking blood. I mean, I hate drinking blood. How do I explain that to my people? How does one explain one's love and one's hatred? Isn't loving enough? Isn't loving an explanation in itself?'

The two girls kept staring at each other in silence for a long time. Two misfits brought together by an almost tragedy. Two deviants delighted to have found one another.

'Well …' Ms Tara Musca broke the silence. 'I really think I should suck the sugar syrup on your body and help you clean up.'

They both broke into a loud, spontaneous laughter.

From that day onwards, Ms Tina Quito and Ms Tara Musca needed no one else. They had found each other. That was more than enough. That was all

they needed. While other mosquitoes went seeking blood, Ms. Tina Quito was with Ms. Tara Musca looking for bright coat-button daisies for Ms. Tara Musca to wear. While other houseflies perched on stuff and rubbed their legs, Ms. Tara Musca basked in the sunlight with Ms. Tina Quito, debating the pros and cons of drinking blood. No wonder, both of them found no pros for drinking blood.

'I'm so happy I'm a housefly,' Ms. Tara Musca teased Ms. Tina Quito. 'I can never drink blood. I don't know how you all do it!'

'I really wish you houseflies had blood,' Ms. Tina Quito looked at Ms. Tara Musca in anger. 'I'd have sucked all blood out of your body.'

'You? Suck blood?' Ms. Tara Musca teased Ms. Tina Quito again.

Then Ms. Tara Musca flew away and Ms. Tina Quito chased her. And then Ms. Tara Musca ran out of breath.

'Stop! Stop!' Ms. Tara Musca huffed and puffed.

'Caught ya!' Ms. Tina Quito landed right on top of Ms. Tara Musca, toppling her coat-button daisy.

'I'll wear this flower now,' Ms. Tina Quito told Ms. Tara Musca. 'Get up. How do I wear this?'

SWEETS
SWEETS
Mithai

And they became friends again.

Coat-button daisies, sunlight, fights and patch-ups, their togetherness despite their differences, and one other thing they couldn't live without: sugar syrup. All kinds of sugar syrup.

They flew from eatery to eatery, mithai shop to mithai shop, restaurant to restaurant, just to sample all the various kinds of sugar syrup they could find.

There was the plain, basic sugar syrup that went with any and all mithai.

There was the thick, really sugary sugar syrup that went with the unforgettable golden gulab jamun, and which tasted like heaven when it was fresh and hot.

There was the fragrant, mixed-with-rose-water sugar syrup that was used with rich, fluffy rasgullas.

Their days were filled with sugar syrup, and conversation. The two friends talked about everything. Their lives, families, struggles. They bitched about the people they had disappointed and got into fights with as they tried to defend their choices.

***

One day, Ms Tina Quito and Ms Tara Musca flew into a *mithai* shop to try the sugar syrup there. There were hot *jalebis* being pulled out of a *kadhai* and put into warm, thick sugar syrup. Just the kind of view that the two friends longed for nearly all the time.

'Hey, Tina!' Ms Tara Musca had already dashed off towards the jalebis as she spoke to Ms Tina Quito. 'I really cannot hold myself back any longer. Join me at the jalebis.'

'Tara! Tara! Careful! There are humans close by. Let them disperse first.'

Ms Tina Quito called out to her friend, but to no avail. Ms Tara Musca had already flown and sat at the edge of the stainless-steel tub into which the freshly prepared jalebis, covered with sugar syrup, were being transferred. Ms Tara Musca was, in fact, already greedily gobbling up the sugar syrup.

Ms Tina Quito laughed.

'The two of us!' she thought. 'Crazy about sugar syrup!'

And then she spotted something that wiped the smile off her face and froze her to the core.

A human male, huge, fearsome, had gone and stood by Ms Tara Musca, who was too engrossed in the sugar syrup to notice any trouble approaching her. The human lifted his right hand and took position to crush Ms Tara Musca.

'TAAAA ARAA AAA...'

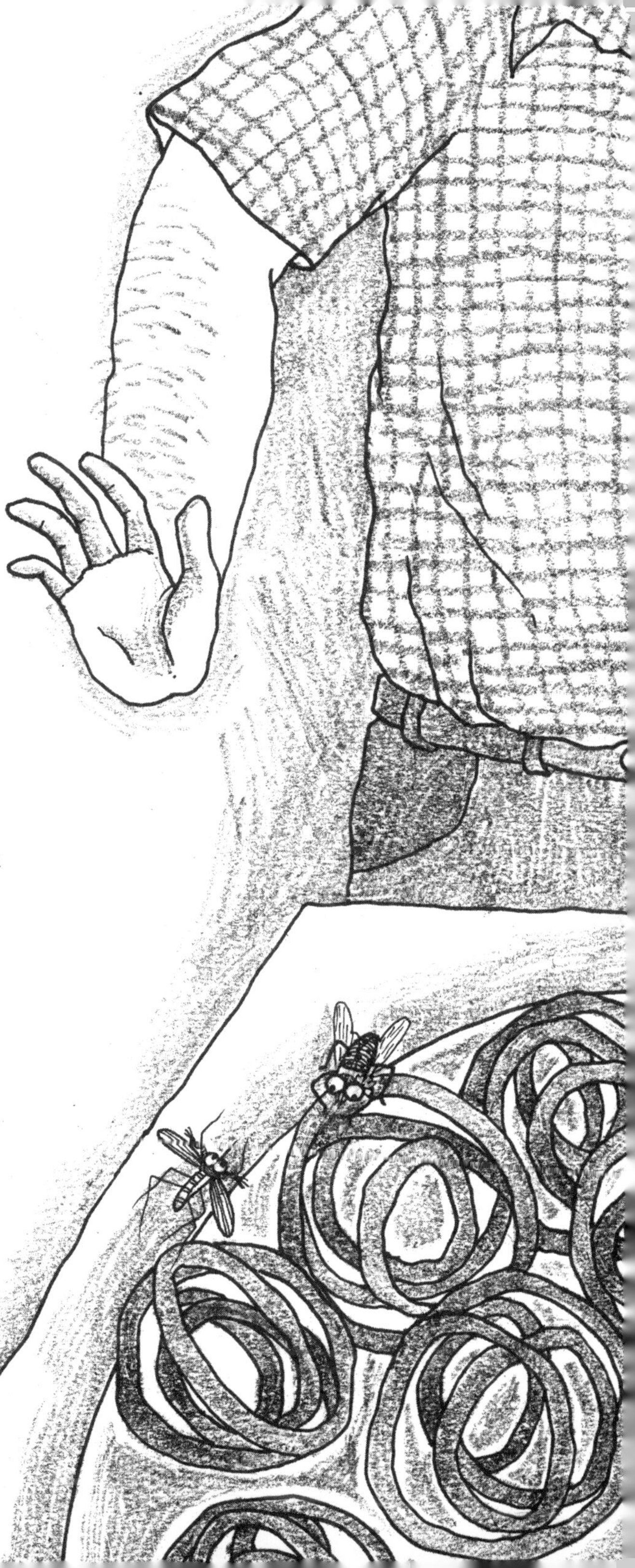

Ms Tina Quito shouted her friend's name. But her voice was lost in the din of the shop.

The human's hand was dropping closer to Ms Tara Musca's body. There was no way she could fly away to safety in time.

Ms Tina Quito knew she had to act fast, act right away.

As the human's hand inched dangerously close to Ms Tara Musca's body, Ms Tina Quito jabbed her sharp, needle-like proboscis into his left eye. And as fast as she had jabbed, she flew out equally fast and backwards, several feet away, to a point of safety.

The human wasn't as fast as Ms Tina Quito. Instead of hitting Ms Tara Musca with his right hand, he used that hand to slap whoever had jabbed him in the eye. He only ended up hurting himself. Ms. Tara Musca, alert now, escaped.

Ms Tina Quito flew to Ms Tara Musca.

'Are you okay?' she asked.

Ms Tara Musca saw the human rubbing his eye and understood what had happened.

'Did you just jab or did you also drink?' she asked Ms Tina Quito.

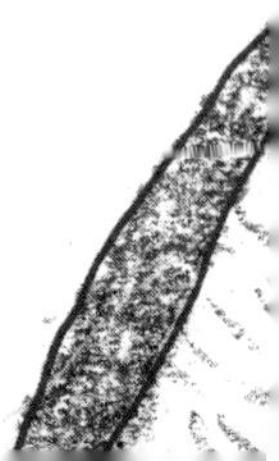

'Yuck!' Ms Tina Quito pretended to puke. 'You really think I'm going to drink the blood of that odious creature? I have my standards, you know. I'm fully into sugar syrup now.'

Teeheeheehee ...

Ms Tara Musca laughed so hard, the coat-button daisy nearly fell off her head.

'Careful! Careful! The flower!'

Ms Tina Quito leaned closer to her friend and fixed the coat button daisy on her head.

Then Ms. Tina Quito lifted a leg and Ms. Tara Musca too lifted one, while they were still mid-air, and they slapped their legs together.

'Time to look for a different place, sister,' Ms. Tara Musca said. 'I don't like the vibes here.'

'The vibes, of course,' Ms. Tina Quito made a face. 'You first get into trouble yourself and then blame the vibes at that place!'

'Oh, very fine!' Ms. Tara Musca shot back. 'And who had been drowning in sugar syrup one day?'

'Ah! I don't remember bad things,' Ms. Tina Quito said. 'I'm a positive being.'

'Yes, of course!' Ms. Tara Musca said. 'Don't tell me!'

And then, squabbling, but flying very close to one another, they flew towards the river Sorna.

*****

ACKNOWLEDGEMENTS

Thank you to my family, from where the stories came
Thank you, Jayapriya Vasudevan and Jacaranda, for championing my works
Thank you, Westland Books, for having me on your shelves
Thank you, Proiti Roy, for adorning my words with your brilliance
—Sowvendra